BUSTED

JEAN MILLS

ORCA BOOK PUBLISHERS

Published in Canada and the United States in 2026 by Orca Book Publishers.

Library and Archives Canada Cataloguing in Publication
Title: Busted / Jean Mills.
Names: Mills, Jean, 1955- author
Series: Orca anchor.
Description: Series statement: Orca anchor
Identifiers: Canadiana (print) 20250118734 | Canadiana (ebook) 20250118742 | ISBN 9781459840508 (softcover) | ISBN 9781459840515 (PDF) | ISBN 9781459840522 (EPUB)
Subjects: LCGFT: Novels.
Classification: LCC PS8576.I5654 B87 2026 | DDC jC813/.54—dc23

Library of Congress Control Number: 2024952985

Summary: In this high-interest accessible novel for teen readers, Jonah inadvertently records a video of two of his hockey teammates play fighting. When one of them is seriously hurt, Jonah is conflicted about what to do.

Orca Book Publishers is committed to reducing the consumption of nonrenewable resources in the production of our books. We make every effort to use materials that support a sustainable future.

Orca Book Publishers gratefully acknowledges the support for its publishing programs provided by the following agencies: the Government of Canada, the Canada Council for the Arts and the Province of British Columbia through the BC Arts Council and the Book Publishing Tax Credit.

Design by Ella Collier.
Edited by Gabrielle Prendergast.
Author photo by Trina Koster.

Printed and bound in Canada.

29 28 27 26 • 1 2 3 4

CERTIFIED CANADIAN PUBLISHER

ORCA BOOK PUBLISHERS
orcabook.com

Chapter One

"Shoot it!" Drake yells.

I wind up and shoot the puck as hard as I can from the blue line.

I miss the net completely. The puck bounces off the boards and back out in front of the goal. And Drake is ready. He gets it on his stick and makes no mistake. One quick flick of his wrist and the puck is in the net behind Carter.

"Goooooooal!"

Drake does his best NHL-style goal celebration, pretending he just won the Stanley Cup. And we let him, because that's just Drake.

Coach blows his whistle, and we all circle in for his wrap-up.

"Nice job, boys. See you tomorrow. It's our last game before the Intercity Tournament starts on Saturday. Only one more practice, on Thursday, but I think we're ready."

He points at Drake and Carter.

"Remember, a couple of scouts are coming on Saturday, so it's time to show them your stuff, right?"

Drake is our leading scorer, and Carter has more shutouts than any other goalie in the U18 league, even though they're both only sixteen.

No surprise that the scouts are lining up to watch them.

"So off you go," Coach says. "Make it fast, eh? I have to be somewhere tonight, and I don't want to be waiting for sweaty teenage boys to get out of the dressing room. Got it?"

"Got it, Coach," we all say, grinning. He says this after every game. Usually he stands just outside the dressing-room door, talking on his phone as if he has all the time in the world.

We skate off the ice and clomp down the hallway to our dressing room.

"Nice miss there, bud," says Drake, giving me a shove as we come through the door. "Good thing I was there for the rebound."

"Oh, I meant to do that," I say. "It was a setup. Of course, Carter gave you the whole stick side."

"I did," says Carter. He's already sitting on the bench undoing his goalie pads. "Just wanted to give you a gift, Drake." He looks up and smiles. "I know you need a little help finding the back of the net."

Drake swears at him. That friendly kind of swearing that means he isn't really mad.

And then he looks over at Carter and says, "Hey, want to settle this? Old style?"

The room gets quiet.

I've been looking down at my phone because it's my job to start the music. Yes, I'm the team DJ. I have all the playlists. The "We Won!" playlist. And the "Road Trip" playlist.

And the "After-Practice Chill" playlist, which is the one I'm looking for right now.

But when Drake says that to Carter, I look up. Everybody looks up. Some of us glance at the door. It's propped open, just a little. That's the rule. Coaches don't have to be in the room, but they have to be there. At the door. On duty.

So we know Coach is standing right there. I lean forward a little and I can see him. Of course, he's on his phone, earbuds in. He's not paying attention to us and what's happening.

I kind of wish he was, though.

Carter has taken off his sweater, pads and skates. He's sitting there in his sweaty undershirt and hockey pants. "What? You mean boxing?"

Drake grins. He has his skates and shoulder pads off. "Sure. Why not?"

"Because it's against the rules," says Alex, sitting beside Drake.

"Who cares about rules?" says Drake, looking around. "Coach doesn't. If he did, he'd be standing at the door right now watching us. This is our room, and we can make our own rules. And hey, it's fun, right?"

Drake is in a mood, I can tell. He gets like this sometimes. We've all seen it.

He has fun being a badass. He's the guy who will give that extra hit on the ice. He'll put his stick where it shouldn't be and make a guy fall. It's all part of the game to him, like the guys we watch on TV. I guess it makes him feel good to be the strongest. To get the other team mad at him.

Okay, yes. He's a really, really good hockey player. He will probably make it to the NHL.

But we all know he has a wild streak too. He likes to break the rules. On the ice. And off the ice.

Like right now.

It's clear to everyone in the room that he wants to have a fight with Carter. We used to do this a lot. Helmets and gloves. Go at it for a few minutes. Somebody gives in, and it's over. No harm, no foul.

Okay, maybe the odd bruise or two.

But parents, or somebody, heard about it

and told the people who run the league it had to stop. So it stopped.

Or so they think.

"Come on," Drake is saying to Carter. Staring at him. Grinning, and not in a funny way. "You know you want to smash me."

"I do," says Carter. "But I don't want to get smashed."

The rest of us are watching this and glancing at the door. Coach has moved away now, and I can't even see him.

Drake stands up and grabs his helmet and gloves.

"Come on, just a quick one before Coach comes back. Show me how mad you are at me for scoring on you," he says and laughs.

Then he turns to me. "Let's get that music going, DJ Jonah! Come on. A little fight music."

I glance at Carter, and he's putting his cage back on. He shrugs at me.

"Can I borrow your gloves?"

"Sure," I say and throw them at him. "No blood, please."

And then I look at my phone, scroll to the "Game Time" playlist and hit *play*. Right away the music starts, and I crank it up. The Bluetooth speaker vibrates, it's so loud.

I look up. Carter and Drake are standing now, kind of dodging a bit. Pretending to be warming up. Carter laughs at Drake doing some weird muscle-flexing thing, and it's such a great moment, I can't help it. I turn on my camera and take a picture of them.

Yeah, yeah, I know I'm not supposed to. Phones in the dressing room are for music only, and I promised Coach that's all I would use it for.

But it's such a perfect moment. Two guys, suited up and ready for a fight. Goofing around and making it look like a big deal.

Only, I don't realize until later that I don't just take a picture.

Holding my phone on my knee, not really thinking about it, I film a video.

Chapter Two

Yes, I film a video. With sound. In fact, there might be more sound than actual video, but it's there.

A video of Carter turning to say something to Alex. And Drake choosing that exact moment to punch Carter so hard in the ribs that Carter drops to the floor. He curls up in a ball, moaning.

"Come on, wuss. Quit faking it," says Drake, bouncing up and down like a boxer ready to go. "It wasn't that hard."

"I don't think he's faking," says Jasper. "You okay, Carter?"

"I wasn't ready," Carter manages to say. And then he moans a little more.

The room gets quiet.

"Come on." Drake sounds mad now. Maybe scared?

"Can't breathe," says Carter. "It hurts."

Crap. This is real.

"Get your gloves off, quick!" Drake says to him. "And your helmet!"

What's going on? Carter is lying there in pain, and Drake is worried about getting his gloves and helmet off?

He throws his own gloves over to the bench and tosses off his helmet. Alex and

Jasper come over to help Carter with his helmet. Alex tosses my gloves back at me.

Carter is trying to roll over.

"Oh, crap. That hurts," he says, sitting up. His eyes are closed, and he's wincing.

"What the hell is going on here, guys?"

It's Coach. He just came in the door, and we didn't even notice.

And that's when I glance down to turn off the music.

And that's when I see that I was recording a video. I turn it off too.

Okay, this is bad.

Taking pictures of guys in the dressing room is something the league doesn't like. Especially if pictures show up on social media or get shared. The parents don't like it either. Some guys don't care. I guess they think they look all big and tough. I know I wouldn't want the world to see me in my underwear. So, yeah, there are rules.

And I just broke them. *Oops.* Time to get changed and get out of here.

"What's going on?" Coach asks again. "Carter? What happened?"

Silence as we all look around at each other. Is Carter going to tell Coach that he and Drake were boxing? Even though it's against the rules?

We all know why it's against the rules. The rule is there so people don't get injured. Kind of like Carter is injured right now.

If Coach finds out, he'll probably bench both of them. Or worse. He could suspend them. And how can we even hope to compete at the tournament without Drake, our leading scorer, and Carter, our star goalie?

And what about the scouts...?

"I fell, Coach," says Carter. "Tripped. Landed on the bench. I think I cracked a rib or something. It hurts."

I look over at Drake. His face relaxes, just a little. He's almost smiling.

Of course he's smiling. He just avoided being busted.

"Okay, can you sit up?" Coach bends down to help him. Alex steps in too.

They get Carter standing and help him to his spot in the dressing room.

"Get changed, guys," Coach says over his shoulder to the rest of us. "And get out of here."

Carter is trying to take deep breaths, but we can see it hurts.

"Your dad's outside," says Coach. "Maybe we'll get him in here." He turns to me because I'm changed and ready to leave. "Jonah, go get Carter's dad, please."

"Okay." I glance around the room as I pick up my bag and stick. Most of the guys are watching Carter and Coach. Except for Drake.

He's stuffing his shoulder pads into his hockey bag. He glances up and shrugs at me, but I just ignore him.

I've never been happier to leave the dressing room.

Chapter Three

My dad is in the parking lot, waiting to drive me home.

"Good practice?" he asks.

"Yeah," I say. "The usual."

Wow, it was not the usual. But there's no way I'm going to tell him about Drake and Carter and the fight. Or the video of the fight.

Crap. What was I thinking?

I wasn't thinking. I was just holding my

phone and accidentally pressing the video button.

I'd like to pull out my phone and watch the video I recorded. I want to see just how bad it is, but I can't do that here in the car. Instead Dad and I talk about the Leafs vs. Bruins game that will be on TV tonight.

"Homework first, right?" says Dad.

"Yup," I say.

I don't tell him my "homework" includes watching a video of Drake beating Carter up in the dressing room.

When we get home, I spread out my grubby hockey gear on the drying rack in the garage. My mom made this rule when I was just a little kid on my first team.

"No smelly sports gear in my house, please!" she said.

My mom is cool. She's also the boss, and we all know it.

I like it, to be honest. I don't mind someone having rules and making sure we all follow them.

Maybe I should introduce Drake to my mom. Following rules is something Drake is not good at.

Sure, he knows the rules of hockey. He knows how to avoid an offside call. He knows he can't cross-check the other team's goalie. Getting a penalty would hurt the team. But elbowing a guy when the refs aren't looking? That sends a message. And Drake's message on and off the ice has always been *I'm tough. You can't hurt me.*

Yeah, that's Drake. He makes his own rules.

I finish hanging my gear on the rack and open the back door to go inside. I can hardly wait to get to the privacy of my room and pull out my phone. Actually, I already have my phone out as I step into the back room and close the door behind me.

And then I nearly fall over in surprise because someone is standing right there.

It's Liv, my sister.

"So I hear there was some excitement after practice today," she says.

Liv and I look alike. That's because we're twins. She even keeps her hair short, like mine. Hers is stylish and fluffs out. Mine is not stylish and just hangs there. We're both pretty tall too. And we're both into sports. Hockey for me, tennis for her. We're friends, which is better than other brothers and sisters I know.

She's also very smart. At school she always gets better marks than I do. And she's smart in other ways too. That's what makes me nervous right now.

I take a quick look past her to see if our parents are nearby. Nope.

"I have no idea what you're talking about," I say.

Of course I know what she's talking about. And I know how she knows. She and Carter have been kind of circling each other for weeks.

She thinks he's hot. I'm glad he hasn't told me what he thinks of her. But I have a feeling they are working their way toward being a couple.

I was fine with it. But right now I'm not so sure.

I don't look at her. I just walk by her toward my room as if there's nothing to talk about.

"Right," she says as she follows me.

"Go away," I say at the door of my room.

"Right," she says again and walks in right behind me before I can block her.

There's no escape when Liv has her mind made up.

"Tell me," she says.

I go over to my desk and try to look busy, plugging my phone into the charger.

"Tell you what?" I'm trying to play it cool. Make it look like I don't know what she's talking about.

"Hey, Jonah? Don't ever go into the spy business," she says. "You suck at it."

"Truth."

"Carter texted me," she says. Big surprise.

But nobody knows about the video, I tell myself. Right?

"Come on, tell me what happened. It sounds juicy." She flops onto my bed.

I sit down at my desk and think fast.

Okay, she knows about the fight. Fine.

But she doesn't know about the video. Even Carter doesn't know I recorded the whole thing. Nobody knows.

Nobody but me.

So I decide to take the easy route. Tell her what she knows already and keep the rest to myself.

"Yeah, the usual," I say. "Drake being Drake. Pounding on Carter a little too hard."

"Carter says it hurts. A lot," she says. "Drake is such a jerk. Why didn't your coach stop it?"

"Coach had a phone call. He was just outside the door," I say. Was he? I'm not sure about that. "He came in just after it happened."

Okay, that's not good. I wonder if Coach will be in trouble for that.

Coach will be in a lot more trouble if anyone finds out what really happened. But only the guys in that room know.

Well, the guys and Liv now.

Crap. I don't like the way this is shaping up.

"You could have stopped it," says Liv. "Why didn't you?"

"I was on my phone," I say. *Wait, that's probably not a good thing to say.* "I was—I was picking the playlist."

"Oh, right. Your DJ job in the dressing room," she says and shakes her head. "Nerd."

"It's my job. What can I say?" I shrug.

"Are you sure you weren't taking pictures?" she asks.

I try to look offended. "Of course not! That's against the rules." But I don't look at her when I say it. She already knows I'm not good at lying.

"Hmmm. Right," she says. "Drake is such a goon sometimes. Poor Carter."

"Well, I hope he's okay for the game. We need him, and Coach says there are going to be scouts there to watch," I say. I open a desk drawer and pretend to be looking for something. "So can I have some privacy now, please?"

"Hmmm," says Liv. I know that voice. She can tell from the way I'm avoiding her that there's more.

Suddenly Mom yells from the kitchen.

"Jonah! You left your backpack in the garage!"

I must have been so distracted while putting my hockey gear out that I forgot it.

"Just a sec," I yell back.

"Now!" yells Boss Mom. "I just tripped on it!"

Fine.

"Out, please?" I hustle Liv out the door and head down to the kitchen. Mom is pulling something out of the oven and Dad is setting the table.

I go out through the back door and into the garage. Yup, there's my backpack. It's lying on the garage floor right where I dropped it when I came in with my hockey bag.

I sling it over my shoulder and make my way through the kitchen back to my room. Liv is gone when I get there, thank goodness. I go in and close the door behind me.

And then I grab my phone and open the video.

Chapter Four

Okay, I'm not going to win an Academy Award for this video. I did a terrible job of recording the action. But I didn't know I was recording the action, did I?

It's bad. It starts with Drake and Carter in their fight gear, ready to go. That was the picture I thought I was taking.

Drake is so much bigger than Carter. There he is, flexing his arms like one of those Ultimate Fighting Championship guys.

Carter laughs. They throw a few fake punches at each other. They laugh some more.

And then Carter turns to say something to Alex and Drake hits him. He hits Carter low. In the ribs.

The image tilts down then. I'd thought I had taken a photo and didn't realize I was still filming. But I was still filming.

I see the floor. Carter's legs as he lies there. Somebody else's feet. Maybe Jasper? Alex?

But the worst part is the sound. The sound is as clear as anything.

Carter moaning. Drake saying, "Come on, wuss. Quit faking."

Jasper saying, "I don't think he's faking."

The whole thing is there. Getting their gear off. Coach coming in.

"What's going on here?"

The end.

Yup. The video is pretty bad. Lots of floor. And feet. It's a terrible video.

But the soundtrack is clear. It's all there for anyone to hear.

"Crap." I say it out loud. I can't help myself.

So what do I do? Nobody can see this. We'd all be in such trouble. Coach would be in trouble. Our team could be kicked out of the tournament. Fighting in the dressing room? For fun?

Yeah, this is bad. Especially for Carter. He got hurt. But it's bad for Drake too. I've known him since we were little kids. He likes to look tough, and sometimes he gets in trouble at school. Nothing terrible. That time he stole the girls' basketball at recess. Or when he climbed on the school roof on a dare. But he's a great hockey player, and he loves the game.

Breaking the rules and hurting a teammate isn't great, though.

Getting suspended from a tournament isn't great either. Especially now that we know scouts are coming to check him out.

If he finds out I filmed the fight, that would not be good for me or anyone.

So, of course, I delete it.

I feel better right away. It's done. It's gone.

After supper I do my homework and go downstairs to watch the Leafs vs. Bruins game on TV. It's always a battle when these two teams play each other.

"Whoa!" Dad yells at the TV. "Penalty! High-sticking!"

Two players drop their gloves and start fighting. Yup. Just a regular Leafs vs. Bruins game.

"Here we go," says Dad. "These guys can't play a game without dropping the gloves and punching each other."

Suddenly I have a clear image in my head of Drake and Carter with their helmets and gloves on. The punch. Carter falling to the floor.

"Yeah, I know," I say. But I'm not really thinking about those NHL players on the TV screen.

My phone buzzes, and I look down. One of the guys has posted in our team group chat.

Looks like our dressing room

A few guys post emojis of laughing faces.

Drake could beat both of them

More laughing faces. Nothing from Drake, though.

Anybody heard from Carter? someone asks.

There's a long pause, so I look up at the game again. The players from the fight are now sitting in their penalty boxes. They call to each other. They have big smiles on their faces. It looks like they're having the most fun ever.

"I sure hope your games don't turn into this kind of stupidity," Dad says.

Uh, Dad? It's not the games you have to worry about, I say silently.

After a few minutes my phone buzzes again.

It's Carter. Another post.

Bruised rib. Doctor says I can't play. Sorry guys.

Everybody jumps in the chat then to tell him how much that sucks. To get better soon.

Still nothing from Drake. No "Sorry" or "That fight was a bad idea."

I feel bad for Carter.

But I also have a feeling I should say something to Drake. He has so much pure skill. I wish I could do some of the things he does with the puck. But he's so rough sometimes too. So physical, and not in a good way. Like he thinks that's what everyone expects from him. Maybe it comes from being so much bigger than everyone else. It's what he sees from some of the big players in the NHL. And his dream is to be there one day. So if someone checks him hard, he has to check them even harder. Too hard, sometimes.

Sort of like he did in a friendly fight with Carter.

Maybe I'll talk to him tomorrow. Maybe...

"Wow, here they go again," says Dad, and I look up at the TV. Two more players are yelling at each other. The refs try to keep them apart.

"Looks like a lot of fun," says Liv from the doorway.

She looks at me with her eyes wide and a big smile on her face. I know what she's really saying. She's saying it looks like the same kind of fun my team had in the dressing room this afternoon.

My phone buzzes again, and I look down. It's a text from Drake.

Not to our group chat. A message just for me.

DON'T SHOW IT TO ANYONE

Show what?

And then I see it, just above his message. The video of the fight, texted to him.

But wait. I didn't send it, so how...?

"Something good?" Liv asks from the doorway.

I look up at her.

You didn't. I don't say it out loud because I don't want Dad to clue in.

She shrugs. *Yup.*

She must have searched my phone when I went out to get my backpack. Found the video. Went to Messages, found Drake's name and sent it.

That's what I get for sharing my password with a sister who is also my tech help desk.

"I'm going to call Carter about a homework question," she says and walks out.

My phone buzzes.

GOT IT? NOBODY SEES THAT VIDEO OR

Drake ends his message there, but I know exactly what he means.

Or I'm going to hurt you.

Chapter Five

I stare at Drake's message and feel sick. This guy is a mess, and I'm part of the reason.

The first thing I want to do is go find Liv and yell bad words at her, but of course I don't.

Right now the most important thing is to calm Drake down so he doesn't beat up somebody at school tomorrow. Somebody meaning me.

I also don't want Coach to find out about it. I would be in big trouble for filming the fight. But Drake and Carter would be in even bigger trouble. Our team could be suspended. We might not be able to play in the tournament. Drake, Carter—the scouts are coming to see them. We need this tournament.

So nobody else can see this video. Nobody can find out about the fight.

I think fast. The truth is always the best choice, right? I text Drake.

I made the video by accident. Sent it by accident when I was trying to delete it

Okay, the last part is not true. But I'm not going to bring Liv into this.

I can see that he read the message. He doesn't reply, so I send another text.

Let's be chill. Just delete it

Long pause. Then I can see he's typing something.

Ok

Okay. Nobody else will see the video. And nobody will talk about it, including me. And Liv wouldn't say anything, would she? I'll have to talk to her...

"Goal!" yells Dad, making me jump.

"Yay! Finally!" I say, pretending I've been paying attention.

For the rest of the night I watch the game, then get ready for bed and try not to think about tomorrow.

I don't sleep very well.

Tuesday morning comes. No sign of Liv at breakfast.

"She left early. Said she had a meeting or something," says Mom.

Sure she did. Probably avoiding me. But I'm so tired I hardly pay attention. I don't know how I'll get through the day.

Drake wakes me up pretty quickly, though.

He comes to my locker and stands very close to me. I have a terrible feeling he's going to bodycheck me right there in the hallway.

"What the hell was that?" he says in a low voice.

"Look, it was a mistake. I know," I say without looking at him. I just keep unloading my backpack. "But we're the only ones who saw it. Carter will stick to his story about falling. Just relax."

"Yeah, relax. Right."

"Let it go, bud," I say.

I glance at him. His face scares me a little. He looks so angry. Drake is not in the mood to "let it go" right now. The tournament, scouts—everything he dreams of. I get it.

"That video better not show up anywhere else," he says. "Or someone is going to be very sorry."

He shoves me hard against my locker before he walks away. People around us turn and stare, first at him, then at me. Everyone wants to know what's going on. Should I tell them my teammate is losing it?

At the lunch break we all show up in the gym for ball hockey. It's something we do every Tuesday at lunchtime, and it's usually fast and fun.

But today it's more like fast and furious. And Drake is the furious. He runs after anyone with the ball and makes contact. He throws an elbow at Jasper when they both go for the ball. He shoves me off-balance just as I'm getting ready to shoot. I fall hard.

Mr. Virani is the gym teacher in charge. Usually he just stands on one side and lets us play, but now he blows his whistle. Loudly.

"Hey! Drake! Cut it out!" he yells. "You okay, Jonah?"

"I'm fine," I say, getting back to my feet.

I look at Drake and mouth, *What the hell, bud?*

He looks at me, and I think he's going to say *Sorry* or something. But he doesn't. He just turns away.

He walks away, throws his hockey stick to the floor and leaves the gym.

Everything goes silent for a moment.

"Wow. He's mad about something," says Alex in a low voice.

"Okay, guys," Mr. Virani calls. "That's it for today. Sorry." And he heads out the door after Drake.

I feel sick. This thing is getting uglier and uglier. If Drake can't control himself on a gym floor, what's he going to be like on the ice?

"He shoved me at my locker this morning,"

I tell Alex in the changeroom. The room is noisy, so nobody else can hear us.

"He walked right by me without even saying anything," says Alex. "Usually he gives me a high five or something."

"I know," I say. "It's like he's turned into a dick all of a sudden."

"Well, he's always been a bit of a dick," Alex says.

"True. But he's also a good teammate," I remind him. "You know. Stands up to goons on the ice? Doesn't let the other team push us around?"

"Not such a great teammate today out there," says Alex, nodding toward the gym. "I mean, he nailed you for no reason."

No reason? Maybe I should tell Alex about

the video. No, I tell myself. It's better if no one else knows.

But I can't get Drake's face out of my mind. It's easy to see how angry he is right now. Sometimes on the ice he gets like this too. Angry. Almost violent. Okay, yes, violent.

I don't always know where that anger comes from. But this is different.

Right now this video has him running scared. What can I do? I'm part of the problem.

And that makes me nervous.

"I guess something is bugging him," I say.

"Something like beating up Carter yesterday?" says Alex. "Come on. Drake has issues. You know it. I know it. He gets away with it because he's such a great hockey player."

"He's not always that bad," I say.

"Okay, okay." Alex shrugs. "He's not always that bad. But he's sometimes that bad, right?"

"Yes. Okay. You're right," I say. "I just feel like he needs some help more than anything. Like...he's out of control, you know?"

"I know," says Alex. "Like he might do something—"

"Something stupid," I say.

We pick up our gym bags and head toward the door.

"What did you say?"

Drake is there in the doorway. He must have come back in to get his gym bag, and we didn't see him.

We sure see him now. That angry face. Eyes wide. Fists clenched.

"Uh, hey, Drake..." Alex is about to say more, but Drake doesn't wait.

He just turns and walks out. Alex and I stand there, frozen, as the door closes behind him.

Chapter Six

"What do we do?" Alex asks. "I mean, should we be worried?"

Yes, we should be worried. I've never seen Drake look that mad.

I have to fix this before he does something stupid. And for Drake, "something stupid" might mean hurting someone.

The bell rings for afternoon classes. Alex and I drop our gym bags in our lockers. Then we head to math class.

It's Drake's class too.

"Do you think he'll be waiting for us behind the door or something?" asks Alex as we get close to the classroom.

"No, he's not stupid enough to jump us in front of Mrs. Korr," I say, trying to sound sure of myself. I'm not sure at all.

But he's not there.

In fact, we don't see him at school for the rest of the afternoon.

"What's he doing?" Alex asks me as we get our backpacks at the end of the day. "Hiding? Getting ready to ambush us?"

The thought makes me more nervous. He wouldn't do anything that stupid, would he?

"We'll see Drake at the game tonight," I say.

Do I want to see Drake at the game tonight? I'm not sure.

X

"What's wrong with you? Are you sick?" Liv asks at supper.

I can hardly eat. I keep seeing Drake's face in gym class as he bodychecked me to the floor.

"No, I'm not sick," I say and look over at her. I hope she can understand the look on my face.

You had to send him that video, didn't you? Don't you know that was a terrible idea?

And because we're twins, she gets it. Well, not the exact words, of course. But when I'm carrying my gear out to the car, she comes too.

"Are you going to be okay?" she asks.

We both glance at the back door. Dad hasn't come out yet. We don't want him to hear this conversation.

"Yes," I say. "But Drake is mad. Really, really mad. And it's because he's scared that I'm going to show someone that video."

"The video I sent him," says Liv. "I'm so, so sorry. I didn't want to get you into a mess."

I open the back gate of the car and swing my hockey bag inside.

"Yeah, well, what were you trying to do, Liv? Just having some fun?"

I'm a little mad at her, to be honest. But maybe that's because I'm scared too.

"I'm sorry, Jonah. Really. But..." She pauses.

"But what?"

She shrugs.

"Jonah, I know he's your friend. But Drake needs to change. He's going to hurt someone else. He's already hurt Carter just for fun in some stupid pretend fight. That wasn't pretend. Friends don't hit friends that hard. Hard enough to hurt them."

Ah, right. Carter. Of course Liv is going to defend Carter.

"Yeah, well..."

"Ready to go, bud?" Dad asks as he comes out the door. "You coming too, Liv?"

"No, not tonight," she says. She turns and goes back into the house.

Dad watches her go. He turns to me.

"Everything okay, Jonah?"

"Sure, everything's fine," I say. "She just wanted me to...to say hi to Carter for her."

"Oh, okay."

We listen to a sports show on the car radio and talk about tonight's game. This is good, because it keeps me from thinking about what's going to happen tonight. What's Drake going to do when I come into the changeroom?

Maybe he's just so mad he won't even show up. That could happen, right?

Right.

When I walk into the dressing room, he's there, already changed into his gear. He watches me come in. He leans back against the wall and taps his stick on the floor.

"Hey," I say to him.

He nods at me. No smile, no words. He just keeps tapping his stick on the floor in front of him. It's a bit creepy.

But at least he didn't jump up and punch me. That's good. Of course, Coach is standing right there at the door. He has his phone out, as usual.

Guys come in and glance at Drake, but nobody talks to him. And nobody mentions Carter or the fight, of course.

Usually the changeroom is noisy with everyone talking. Today it's quiet, and that feels weird.

Even Coach notices.

"What's with you guys?" he asks after a few minutes. He looks around the room. We're all getting ready. Lacing up our skates. Pulling on shoulder pads and sweaters. "Come on, guys. Don't tell me you're nervous about tonight's game."

We play the Cougars tonight. We usually beat them, but the games can be rough. They have two really big guys who like to throw checks. Drake loves it, of course, because he loves to throw checks too.

It's always a fast, physical game.

Just what we don't need tonight.

I glance at Drake. He's staring at the floor. *Tap, tap, tap.*

"Guys, I got this," says Tim, our other goalie. "I know Carter usually gets the Cougars games, but I got this, okay?"

Tim is small, but that's all right for a goalie. He's very flexible and quick on his skates. Quick with the blocker and glove. Carter is much bigger than Tim. Carter is good at dealing with crap from big guys in the crease on scoring chances. Tim is good, but he's easy to knock over.

"Hey, we know you do," says Alex.

"We got you," says Jasper.

"Yeah, we're going to protect you—don't worry," I say.

Other guys join in, and the room gets noisy. Everyone wants Tim to know we're here for him. I think maybe he's a bit nervous.

Drake still doesn't move or say anything. Just *tap, tap, tap*.

It's like listening to a bomb about to go off.

Alex and I look at each other. I know we're thinking the same thing. *What's with Drake?*

"Guys, just go out there and play your game," Coach says. He has no idea that we're all worried about Drake and his weird mood. Of course, he has no idea about the fight either. "Play the structure we've practiced. Don't let their big guys bully you. We're a much faster team."

He looks around the room, and we nod in agreement. He's right. We just have to play the way we always play. Fast skating, quick passing, solid back-checking.

And then he looks at Drake. *Tap, tap, tap.*

"Hey, Drake? You good? Ready?"

Drake stands up and looks around the room. He looks at all of us, but he looks at Alex and me the longest. He's not smiling.

"Ready, Coach," he says as he heads for the door. "Come on, guys. Let's kick their asses."

"Come on, guys!" yells Coach. "Let's go!"

"Should we be worried?" Alex asks me quietly as we follow our team out of the dressing room.

"Yes," I say.

Chapter Seven

It's rough right from the start.

On the first play of the game, I get the puck and skate down the wing. And...*bam*!

A Cougars player throws a check that sends me flying. I fall into the boards hard and land on the ice. It doesn't hurt, really. But it sure stops me.

And before I can get up, Drake has cross-checked the guy to the ice.

“Penalty! Number 21 Eagles!” yells the ref, pointing at Drake.

“Ref!” Drake yells. “That check on our guy was too high! It was a cross-check too! I was just—”

“Penalty box,” says the ref, pointing toward the box.

Drake glares at the ref, and we all think he’s going to argue. Or worse, throw a punch. He bangs his stick on the ice in anger and starts skating to the box. One of the Cougars players says something to him as he skates by, and Drake turns. They yell at each other until the refs pull them apart.

“You okay, Jonah?” Coach asks me when I get back to the bench.

"Yeah, I'm fine," I say.

I look across the ice at Drake in the penalty box. He's slumped over, looking down at his skates. I can't see his face. Maybe he's hurt. He looks like he just lost a championship game.

The refs figure out that this is going to be one of those games. They start calling penalties on everything.

Alex reaches for the puck, and a Cougars player falls. Tripping penalty.

One of the Cougars is pushed into the crease and bumps Tim. Goaltender interference.

Jasper races after the puck with one of the Cougars players, and they hit each other. Their guy falls, and we get an interference call.

Coach is trying not to use swear words when he yells at the refs, but a few are slipping out. It doesn't help the mood on the bench.

It also doesn't help that every time Drake goes out on the ice, one of the Cougars players tries to get him mad. They all know Drake is one of the best, but they also know he has a wild side. They know he doesn't mind the physical stuff. Tripping, slashing, interference. Drake has spent most of the game in the penalty box.

"What's going on with you?" Coach asks Drake when he comes back to the bench after yet another penalty. "You're benched. Sorry, bud. But you're not helping the team today."

We can all tell that Coach is trying not to yell at him, but his voice says it all. Drake is not himself. Where's the fast, smart, strong hockey player? It's not this guy sitting beside me, hunched over and staring at his skates.

Alex is sitting on my other side. He leans forward and looks at Drake. Then he nudges me.

"Is he okay?" he asks.

"I don't know," I say. "I really don't know. He's not playing his usual game. And he just seems so distant. Like he's not here."

"Yeah," says Alex. "Let's hope he's not somewhere in his head, plotting revenge on us for talking about him after gym."

I glance at Drake again. He's still slumped over and staring down at his skates. He does not look like someone plotting revenge.

And now the Cougars are leading 5–1 with five minutes to play.

"You okay?" I say to Drake when I come back after a hard shift. I took another hit and didn't touch the puck once. We didn't even come close to scoring.

"Leave me alone," he says in a low voice. "Just leave me alone."

His voice is so low, it's hard to hear him over the arena noise. Out on the ice, the players are skating, shooting, yelling to each other. Parents and fans are cheering in the stands. It's loud in here. Did I hear him right?

"Bud." I lean in so he can hear me. "What? What's going on?"

There's a face-off in the other end, and we actually get a shot on goal. Everyone cheers, but Drake doesn't even notice.

"I'm just so sick of it," he says. His voice is tight and low. I can hardly hear him.

"What?" Did I hear that right? He's sick of hockey?

He looks out at the ice, and even through his fishbowl visor I can see his eyes. They look dead.

"I'm just so damn tired," he says.

"Bud, hey, I know it's been crappy lately. That video—" I start, but he cuts me off.

"The video was crap for sure," he says. He's still staring at the ice. "Worrying if Coach or anyone would see it. If I'd get kicked out. Worrying if Carter was okay."

He looks over at me then.

"But it's like I have to be that guy. The tough guy. All the time." He shakes his head at me, like he doesn't understand it himself. "I hate it."

I don't see Drake, the guy who likes skating fast and hard. Who likes the bodychecks and the rough stuff. The guy who broke the rules and made Carter fight with him. The guy who was so mad at me about that stupid video.

I see Drake, a guy who needs my help.

"Tell someone," I say. "Tell Coach you feel crappy."

He shakes his head. "Can't."

"You can," I say. "I'll tell Coach."

"Don't," he says. Actually, it's more of a growl.

"Okay, okay, but..."

There's a lot of noise as the Cougars get a breakaway. I watch as Tim makes a big save and everyone cheers.

I look back at Drake and nudge him, but he won't look at me.

"Bud, just let me—"

"Shut up, Jonah," he says. "Just shut up and leave me alone."

That might be the scariest thing I've ever heard him say.

Chapter Eight

We lose 7–1. It's brutal. But we still have to go out and do the handshakes after the game. It's a rule in our league. Sportsmanship and all that crap.

Okay, it's not crap. But when you've just been beaten 7–1 by a team that you should be able to beat, it's crap.

"Sorry, guys," says Tim as we skate toward the exit to the changerooms.

"Hey, not your fault," says Alex, and we all join in.

"We didn't do much to help you," I say.

"Well, neither did the refs," Tim says, and we all agree with him. Loudly.

We don't always blame the refs. But today they really did seem to be watching us more closely than normal. Maybe it was because Drake started looking for trouble after that hit on me.

Drake. I look at the guys ahead of me, the guys behind me.

No Drake.

Is he in the changeroom already? Must be.

But no, he and his gear are gone. That means he must have skipped the handshake line. He did the quick change that we all did when we were little kids. Keep the gear on. Change from skates to shoes. Go home in sweaty, smelly hockey gear.

Drake didn't want to talk to anyone. I think about the conversation we had on the bench. Something is definitely wrong.

Coach is at the changeroom door. Yes, he has his phone in hand. Yes, he's texting. The usual.

But then he looks up. "Hey, guys? Can I have a word? Quiet, please."

We weren't exactly being noisy. After a loss like ours, everyone tends to be pretty quiet anyway.

We stop talking and look up at him.

"I've just been in touch with Drake's dad, and Drake's going to take a break from the team this week," he says.

"Why?" asks Tim.

"You know, guys, sometimes we all just need a break," Coach says and shrugs. "Drake needs a break. His dad says he'll be back for the tournament next weekend, and he says Drake wanted you to know. So that's that. Now on to other important things."

I glance at Alex, who is on the bench across from me. I haven't told him about the conversation I had with Drake on the bench.

Later, I mouth. He nods.

"Tough game, but not your fault, Tim," Coach is saying. He goes on to give us the usual pep talk about losing. "Put it behind you." "Next game is a fresh opportunity." "We're a team, and we know what we have to do." Coach stuff.

He stays in the room. A few dads even come in to chat with him, so we just get changed and leave without talking any more about the game. Or about Drake.

Alex and I leave together and walk down the hallway toward the front foyer where our dads will be waiting to drive us home.

"Hey, Drake's a mess," I tell Alex. "He actually said he was 'tired.'"

"Tired? You mean not enough sleep?" Alex looks puzzled.

"No, I think he meant tired of being the tough guy. All the hitting. Everyone expecting him to be up for the fights," I say. "The Cougars were after him all night."

"Until Coach benched him," says Alex.

I remember the way Drake's face looked as he sat on the bench. Defeated.

"The way he looked tonight, he might have just walked out anyway," I say.

We push the doors open and come into the foyer. It's busy and loud. I see my dad across the room, car keys in hand. He's ready to go.

So am I.

"I wonder if he'll be at school tomorrow," says Alex as I walk away to follow my dad to the car.

"I wonder."

That night I text Drake a few times.

It was a crap game.

You okay?

That Oilers game tonight was sick. McDavid 5 points

No reply. Nothing.

Chapter Nine

He doesn't show up at school on Wednesday or Thursday.

He doesn't show up for practice on Thursday night.

"Is Drake coming tonight, Coach?" asks Alex.

"No," says Coach, and he changes the subject. "Okay, guys. We're going to work on our back-checking tonight."

And that's it.

No texts. Nothing.

Until Friday.

At lunch Alex and I sit at a corner table with Carter and Jasper. I see Liv sitting with some of her friends a couple of tables away. She catches my eye and holds up a chocolate bar. Points at me. *Want some?*

A peace offering, maybe. I shake my head.

"Hey, look," says Alex, and we all turn.

Drake is at the doorway to the lunchroom. He looks around, searching. And then he finds what he's looking for.

Me.

He starts walking toward us.

"Guys," I say to Alex and Jasper. "I don't know..."

I don't know what to expect. Is he finally going to punish me for filming that video?

Or maybe he's going to punch me because he heard me say he's out of control and might do something stupid.

Drake's face is like stone. No emotion. Just his eyes on us.

"He's not going to beat you up in the lunchroom," Alex says.

"I'll protect you," says Jasper.

"And if he does, I'm going to film it," says Carter.

Great. Very helpful.

He comes up to our table and stops.

"Hey," he says to me.

"Hey," I say.

"Can I sit with you guys?"

I realize I've been holding my breath.

"Sure," I say.

He pulls out a chair, sits down and drops his backpack on the floor.

We all wait for him to say something, but he doesn't. He's taking big breaths and looking at the table, not at us.

All very weird.

I look around at the others, and they look back with the same expression. Confusion.

So I decide to turn weird into something less weird.

"Hey, that Oilers game the other night, eh?"

Alex leans forward.

"McDavid. Five points. I mean, what was that?"

Drake looks up at us and nods.

"That was awesome," he says.

We start talking hockey, and it's not weird anymore.

"That breakaway in the second," says Jasper.

"That fifth goal," Carter says, and we all nod in agreement.

We talk hockey and eat our lunches.

Suddenly Liv is standing there. She smiles and offers us pieces of her chocolate bar. Starting with Carter, of course.

"You guys need fuel," she says. "Hockey talk can be very exhausting."

"Thanks," says Carter, smiling at her.

"Thanks," I say, also smiling. I know she's trying to help.

Drake takes a piece. "Yeah. Thanks."

She nods at us, smiles at Carter again and walks back to her table.

"Well, we have chocolate," says Jasper. "Now we need salt."

He reaches into his backpack for a bag of veggie chips and rips it open so we can all have some.

Yes, it's turning into a picnic. Just a bunch of teammates sitting around eating junk food and talking about hockey. Nothing weird about that. It feels good.

I look at Drake. He's listening to Alex talk about the Oilers' scoring statistics and nodding. He looks like...himself. Whatever is going on with him, I think our hockey talk is helping. Also chocolate and chips, of course.

At one point I look over at Liv, and she smiles at me. She's been watching us, I can tell.

Well, she's probably been watching Carter, but that's okay.

When the bell rings, we all pack up and head to math class. Just like any other day.

Drake, Alex and I walk down the hall together.

"So the tournament this weekend," says Drake.

Okay, finally. I've been waiting for this. Maybe this is where he's going to tell us he won't be there.

"Yeah, the tournament," I say. I glance over at Alex, and he raises his eyebrows at me. Neither of us knows what's coming.

"I have a good feeling about it," says Drake. "I hope Coach keeps us on the same line."

"Yeah, me too," I say. "Me too."

I glance at him and he nods at me.

Yup. Drake is back.

Chapter Ten

Saturday morning is our first game in the tournament. Drake scores three goals and sets me up for two more. We win 8–2 over a really strong team.

The handshake line is easy when you win. We head to the dressing room feeling great.

As I step off the ice behind Drake, I see Coach pull him over.

"Couple of scouts out here want to speak

with you and your parents when you're dressed. Okay?"

"Okay," Drake says and looks at me over his shoulder like he just won the Stanley Cup.

I thump him on the back all the way to the dressing room.

"Next stop for this guy is the NHL!" I yell as the two of us come into the room. Of course, no one is surprised. And of course everybody starts yelling at Drake, asking for autographed sticks and free tickets to playoff games.

Yeah, it gets a bit crazy in the best way.

Carter shows up at the door, and the team goes nuts.

"Great win, guys," he says. He turns to Drake. "Man, you were McDavid out there today."

"Thanks. Thanks, I..." he starts. It's like he doesn't know what to say to the guy whose ribs he smashed.

So he says the only thing he can.

"Sorry."

"It's okay, man." They do a bro hug, very gently, of course.

The room is loud, and everyone is excited.

"Music, DJ, please!" yells somebody.

So I pull out my phone and start scrolling.

"Okay, here comes the 'Big Win' playlist for your listening pleasure," I yell and hit *play.*

The music fills the room, and guys make dance moves as they get changed. Coach sticks his head in and laughs at us, and then he turns to talk to someone in the hallway. Maybe the scouts?

"So?" asks Drake, showing off his dance moves in the middle of the changeroom. He leans over so I can hear him better.

"Are you going to film me doing my best moves here, DJ Jonah?"

"Uh, no," I say.

"Well, that's a shame," says Drake. "Sometimes I need to see my moves. You know? See what I'm doing right? See what I'm doing wrong?"

I know exactly what he's talking about. Maybe someday we'll talk about it some more. But not right now.

Right now we're just a couple of hockey bros having fun after a win.

"Your dance moves would set the internet on fire," I say.

"They would," he says with a laugh.

"But hey, you know what that would mean." I point at him. "You'd be famous."

He points right back at me.

"I know. Busted!"

Acknowledgments

A big thank-you to my nephew Eric Mills, a hockey dad and coach, and my great-nephew Matthew Mills, for their experience and suggestions about what hockey boys get up to, on and off the ice. Thank you to the team at Orca Books, especially editor Gabrielle Prendergast for guiding me through this project from pitch to publication.

Jean Mills has been writing since childhood and professionally for over thirty years. Her essays, reviews, features and children's stories have appeared in publications across Canada. She is the author of a number of books for young people, including *Skating Over Thin Ice*, *Larkin on the Shore* and *The Legend*. Her love of hockey inspired her Orca Soundings title *Wingman*. A former college communications professor, Jean loves using her own experiences as an athlete, musician and teacher in her writing. Jean lives in Guelph, Ontario.